Augustine Jones

**Moses Brown: His Life and Services**

A Sketch, Read Before the Rhode Island Historical Society

Augustine Jones

**Moses Brown: His Life and Services**
*A Sketch, Read Before the Rhode Island Historical Society*

ISBN/EAN: 9783337142476

Printed in Europe, USA, Canada, Australia, Japan

Cover: Foto ©Raphael Reischuk / pixelio.de

More available books at **www.hansebooks.com**

# MOSES BROWN:

## HIS LIFE AND SERVICES.

----

## A SKETCH,

READ BEFORE THE

## RHODE ISLAND HISTORICAL SOCIETY,

OCTOBER 18, 1892.

----

### BY AUGUSTINE JONES, LL.B.
Principal of Friends School.

----

PRINTED BY AUTHORITY OF THE SOCIETY.

----

PROVIDENCE: THE RHODE ISLAND PRINTING COMPANY.

*MDCCCLXXXXII.*

At a meeting of the Rhode Island Historical Society, held Tuesday evening, October 18, 1892, Augustine Jones, LL.B., read a Paper on Moses Brown; at the conclusion of which, the following resolution was offered by Mr. Wm. B. Weeden, and, after highly complimentary remarks by Mr. Amasa M. Eaton and President Rogers, was unanimously adopted:

RESOLVED, That the thanks of the Society be, and are hereby presented to Augustine Jones, LL.B., for his able and scholarly sketch of the life and services of Moses Brown, and that a copy of the same be requested for the archives of the Society, that it may serve to honor and perpetuate the memory of one of the founders of this Society, who was an eminent citizen of the State, and an efficient promoter of the cause of education and of humanity.

Extract from the records.

AMOS PERRY, *Secretary.*

———

NOTE.—Letters referred to in this document are nearly all in the Cabinet of the Rhode Island Historical Society.

# MOSES BROWN.

Those gentle, unobtrusive people, who, without seeking the attention and applause of men, have nevertheless contributed to their liberties and their education, and have assisted them to better food and clothing, are now beginning to receive that recognition and appreciation which, until recently, was reserved exclusively for politicians, martial heroes, and demi-gods. These are the true delvers who remove the obstacles from human progress. These are the moral heroes.* It may be said, in

* There is more heroism in self-denial than in deeds of arms.—
*Seneca.*

The true epic of our times is not "Arms and the Man," but "Tools and the Man," an infinitely wider kind of epic.—*Carlyle.*

The time will come when the science of destruction shall bend before the arts of peace; when the genius which multiplies our powers, which creates new products, which diffuses comfort and happiness among the great mass of the people, shall occupy, in the general estimation of mankind, that rank which reason and common sense now assign to it.—*Arago.*

the trite words of Swift, without detracting from
a noble profession, "that whoever can make two
ears of corn, or two blades of grass, to grow upon
a spot of ground where only one grew before, will
deserve better of mankind, and do more essential
service to his country than the whole race of politicians put together."

Industry, invention and education, have fitted
out the cottage with comforts, luxuries and refine-
ments not possible until recently in the homes of
princes. The humblest person by the most unpre-
tending fireside, at a minimum cost, may now
study the wisdom of the ancients, or the marvel-
lous achievements of his own generation.

The city of Providence, fortunate in its situa-
tion at the head-waters of Narragansett Bay,
thrice fortunate in its birth of freedom and soul
liberty in 1636, was most highly favored in the
character and quality of its founders.

But in all that group of sterling, famous men,
who were the colleagues of Roger Williams, not
one was more able, upright and spotless than the
Rev. Chad Brown. And the descendants of that
heavenly minded man have had greater influence
upon the fortunes of this city than the offspring
of any other man living or dead.

Moses Brown, in direct lineage from Chad
Brown, was born in or near Providence, Septem-

ber 23, 1738, and lived here until his death, September 6, 1836, almost ninety-eight years. His long life covered nearly one-half of the existence then, both of the colony and State. He was the youngest son of James and Hope Brown. His brothers were Nicholas, Joseph and John, or as tradition says, the colored servant called them from their sports, "Nickie, Josie, Jonnie, Mosie." Moses Brown survived his brothers many years. He left school at thirteen, having lost his father, and went to live with his uncle, Obadiah Brown, whose daughter, Anna, he married, in 1764. He received considerable property from his uncle, who made his share of his estate the same as that of either of his children. And a further sum also came to him by his marriage. This marriage was blessed by a son and two daughters. The daughter Sarah became the wife of William Almy, in 1794, the other daughter died in infancy. His only son, Obadiah Brown, died in 1822, at the age of fifty-two years, his father surviving him fourteen years.* Obadiah Brown and William Almy were partners with Samuel Slater, the "Father of American Manufactures," thirty years, from 1792 to 1822. They manufactured the first pure cotton goods in this country, under the Arkwright invention.

* See Letter of Noah Worcester, Vol. XIV., p. 287.

The warps were previously linen. And Moses Brown was the foster-parent of the enterprise.

He exhibited in childhood that rare judgment, that fine quality of discrimination in men and things, which distinguished him through life. He took pride in old age in the following illustrative anecdote: A cargo of molasses was being discharged, and the children were allowed with their spoons and bright tin pails to catch the dripping molasses. A customer asked the merchant which was the best cask he had? "I don't know," he replied; "ask that little Mo-sas-us faced Moses Brown; he will tell you."

He was a Freemason, and, indeed, was secretary of the lodge eleven years, until 1769. Then was heard, as all through his life, "Moses Brown will be there at the hour." He was, in 1760, admitted to be a freeman, with full privileges of suffrage.

It marks a change in customs and sentiment, that he was authorized, in 1762, to secure thirty thousand dollars, by lottery, to pave the streets of this city, and that he himself was a director in that lottery. It is not so remarkable, however, when we remember that the best people made use of such means to raise money for churches, or for any other common good. It, however, shows his public spirit.

The Brown brothers were in partnership ten

years, from 1763, and did a very large and successful business.*

Moses Brown lost his wife, Anna, in 1773, when he was thirty-five years of age. He married twice afterwards; first, Mary Olney, in 1779, who died in 1798, Phœbe Lockwood, in 1799, who died in 1808. The last twenty-eight years of his life he was unmarried.

Moses Brown and Stephen Hopkins assisted Joseph Brown in observing the transit of Venus, in 1769. This was done so accurately that the United States Coast Survey has since found the results very satisfactory. Joseph Brown expended five hundred dollars upon this observation, and the location is now called Transit street. Moses Brown had a special taste and aptitude for mathemathics, and, like George Washington, was an accomplished surveyor of land, and possessed an elegant London-made compass.

This same year, 1769, Moses Brown moved the Assembly, of which he was a member, to have the northern line of the State rectified. But Rhode Island had so long neglected her interests, that, although she contended one hundred and fifty years in all, she lost, and Massachusetts gained a district over one-fifth of the present size of Rhode

---

* "Increased means and increased leisure are the two civilizers of man."—*Disraeli.*

2

Island. He was a member of the Committee
which reported the line to the Assembly to be
four miles north of the present boundary.

He represented this town in the Assembly more
than seven years from 1764, at that period when
bitter and strained relations began to exist between
the colony and mother country. There was fierce
strife, also, between Ward and Hopkins, and,
although Hopkins was one of his nearest and
dearest friends, and the Ward faction had reason
to feel that his sympathies were against them, yet,
with a full measure of public confidence, he was
again and again re-elected without opposition.
He was on the most important committees. He
was a member of the committee respecting the
Stamp Act, which, by its resolutions in the interests of Liberty, exceeded in spirit and vigor the
declarations of all sister colonies. They neither
hesitated nor faltered; they said "that the Assembly of Rhode Island has the sole and exclusive
right to lay taxes, and all attempts in that direction by others are unconstitutional." They declared that the officers of the colony were to dis-
regard the Stamp Act, and the colony will indem-
nify and save them harmless."*

* There can be no affinity nearer than our country.—*Plato.*

Of the whole sum of human life, no small part is that which con-

It was in 1770 that Leagues* were formed in
many places against the use of tea. The mis-
tresses of three hundred families in Boston sub-
scribed to such a league, February 9th, binding
themselves not to drink tea until the Revenue Act
should be repealed. And on the 12th the young
ladies of Boston signed one, saying, "We do
with pleasure engage in denying ourselves the
drinking of foreign tea, in hopes to frustrate a plan
which tends to deprive a whole community of all
that is valuable in life." It reveals to us the
intense patriotic sentiments of Moses Brown, his
sturdy character, his obedience to duty, that he
also then made a vow to drink no more tea, and
meekly and quietly kept it more than sixty years,
even to the end of life. He furnished to his guests
always what Samuel Pepys called a "Chinese
drink," of excellent quality, while he drank coffee
or herb tea. "If meat make my brother to offend,
I will eat no flesh while the world standeth."

The burning of the Gaspee, in 1772, was stig-
matized in England by one high in authority, as

sists of man's relations to his country, and his feelings concerning it.
—*Gladstone.*

That grounded maxim, so rife and celebrated in the mouths of
wisest men, that to the public good private respects must yield.—
*Milton.*

*Tea Leagues, 2 Harper's Cyclopedia of United States History,
p. 1376.

"A crime of deeper dye than piracy." And it was suggested that persons from Providence would be sent to England to be tried for their lives, if suspected of a share in it. Governor Hutchinson, of Massachusetts, proposed to annul the charter of the colony. Rhode Island, in her distress, appealed to Samuel Adams. The committee were Darius Sessions, Deputy Governor; Stephen Hopkins, Chief Justice; John Cole, and Moses Brown.*

The characteristic reply of Adams was, that "An attack upon the liberties of one colony, was an attack upon the liberties of all." He was thoroughly sensible, as Franklin was, when he had signed the Declaration of Independence, that they "must hang together, or they would hang separately."

The life and future career of Moses Brown were suddenly and effectively changed, by the death of his wife, Anna, Feb. 5, 1773. He was placed on the committee to correspond with the other colonies, in June, but his feelings, his desires, his heart were changed.† Returning from the grave of

* Bancroft's History of the United States, Vol. VI., p. 441.

† Everything that happens to us, leaves some trace behind; everything contributes imperceptibly to make us what we are.—*Goethe.*

He has himself revealed his political limitations, in a very interesting letter to James Warren, who, after the death of General Joseph Warren, became President of the Provincial Congress of Massachusetts. He writes: "My Religious Principles, thou art, I presume, his wife, and meditating upon the Lord's mercies and favors, and seeking to know what the Divine will was concerning him, he says: "I saw my slaves with my spiritual eyes as plainly as I see you now, and it was given me as clearly to understand that the sacrifice that was called for of my hand was to give them their liberty."* He was "not disobedient unto the Heavenly vision."† He "conferred not with flesh and blood," but on the 10th day of the 11th month, 1773, made the deed of manumission, giving liberty to ten slaves.‡ The deed is duly recorded in the

sensible, do not admit of my interfering in War, but my love for my country, and sense of just rights, is not thereby abated, and if my poor abilities could be any way subservient to a happy change of affairs, nothing on my part would be wanting. I had thoughts of coming to Cambridge, and giving you some account of affairs, and the disposition I found the people in at Boston, having a considerable opportunity with the principal Officers of the Army and Navy, as well as with the Selectmen. But the fatigues of such a disagreeable errand weighed strongly to bring me home to my family and friends, who were anxiously waiting our return."

Providence, 11 of 5 mo., 1775. —*Letters, Vol. II., p. 32.*

*Every duty we omit, obscures some truth we should have known. —*Ruskin.*

There is no evil that we cannot face, or fly from, but the consciousness of duty disregarded.—*Daniel Webster.*

To what gulfs a single deviation from the track of human duties leads!—*Byron.*

† Obedience is the mother of success.—*Æschylus.*

‡ Not the Christian religion only, but Nature herself cries out against the state of slavery.—*Leo X.*

Probate Records, Vol. 6, page 73, and a copy is in the Cabinet of this Society. This document is full of directions to his legal representatives to take care of these wards, who had not been taught to take care of themselves.

It reveals, also, the peculiar religious teachings of the Society of Friends, of that period, although he did not join them until the next year. He says to his slaves, "Be watchful and attentive to that Divine teaching in your own minds, that convinces you of sin, and as you dutifully obey its enlightenments and teachings, it will not only cause you to avoid open sin, * * * but will teach and lead you into all that is necessary for you to know as your duty to the Great Master of all men, for He says, 'I will write it in their hearts, and they shall all know me, from the least to the greatest.'" He became a member of the Society of Friends April 28th, 1774. The committee to visit him report "that they have had an opportunity with him, and think it may be safe to grant his request. Therefore, he is received under the care of the meeting."

This record is certainly tame in the light of his subsequent career in the Society, of which he was for half a century the most distinguished ornament, and the most influential member in New England. Stephen Hopkins was disowned by

Friends, in March, 1773, because he would not liberate a slave woman. He, however, attended the meetings of the Society through life. It is probable that he was annoyed by the officiousness of the committee in meddling with his private affairs, and refused to be dictated to by them. He was certainly always in favor of human freedom. Moses Brown the same year liberated his slaves, and the next year joined the Society which Stephen Hopkins had left.

The Revolutionary War and separation from the mother country probably received little sympathy from Moses Brown. He was not prepared for resistance to blood. There he found his limitation. He was surprised, in 1775, when separation was suggested to him as a possibility. Even Dr. Franklin did not, until the very latest moment, think such extreme results were to follow. Rhode Island, by opposition to impost law, set in motion the agitation which brought forth the Constitution of the United States; and yet she was the last of the original States to adopt it.

It has been said, on excellent authority, that in that critical period, between 1787 and 1790, in which the momentous question of the Union wavered in the balance, the great personal influence of Moses Brown with his fellow-citizens, (although he was in private life,) contributed powerfully towards the ratification of the Constitution by this State.

Silent influence, without annals, has often been more potent in great events, than the incidents with brilliant record, which have taken the name of history.

The once belligerent Moses Brown had become an apostle of peace. The religious change from Baptist opinions and teachings to the views of Friends which he experienced, has been often the subject of comment. He himself related that his first religious interest was awakened in a frightful storm on the bay, when he seemed to stand in the very presence of death. But the loss of his first wife, the liberation of his slaves, and the sympathy received by him from the Society of Friends in this act of justice, his studies, and the natural constitution of his mind, which was of a deeply contemplative nature, all contributed to direct him to that field where his eminent Christian course of usefulness and true nobility of soul were to be most intimately known and felt.

Not a Friend in the world held slaves in 1776, the era of the Declaration of Independence.

His brother John, or as he called him "Brother John," the chief rebel connected with the destruction of the Gaspee, was captured on his own cargo of flour, April 22, 1775, and taken by the British to Boston as a prisoner. Moses, the Quaker, followed him to Boston, carrying nineteen letters of noted people, to aid his expedition, the purpose of which was to save John, who was in great peril. It has long been a difficult question what means and methods such a good man could have used to rescue his brother, when John was the very man, the exact fugitive from justice the English had been searching for during three years, with great vigilance and cost.

It is very gratifying that Moses Brown has himself narrated frankly his proceedings in the extrication of " Brother John," and thereby removed all possible doubt, if there ever was any, of his own simple honesty and integrity in what he said and did in Boston for his release.* The account of this adventure is in a letter to Tristam Burges, now in the archives of this Society, bearing date January 12th, 1836, written only nine months before his own death, and it assists us to fix the date of the capture of John, if we bear in mind that it was three days after the skirmish at Lexington. The British were in the city of Boston,

---

* The fine conscientiousness, strict good faith and honor of Moses Brown in this affair, appear in his letter to John three days before the Battle of Bunker Hill, entreating him to live up to the promises which had secured his release in Boston.—*Letters, Vol. II., p. 35;* see also the *Answer of John Brown, p. 36.*

and the Americans were besieging it. He passed
the American lines successfully with his letters;
he next encountered the British sentinel, who did
not see him until he was near to him, and then
he says, " When he turned and saw me near him,
he was so angry that he gave me such a blast as
I never had, or heard before. I did not know
what his fright might induce him to do." They
were both thoroughly frightened; but soon his
letters took him to General Gage, to Admiral
Graves, to Chief Justice Oliver, and also to visit
" Brother John." He was the very first American who had gone into Boston after the contest at
Lexington, and while he waited for General Gage
he conversed with Major Pitcairn, who convinced
him that he thought the Americans fired first at
Lexington. Judge Oliver, who was one of the
Commissioners who held Court in Newport a long
time, directed by his Majesty to find out who
burnt the Gaspee, said to Moses Brown, "It is
true there were named before the Court five John
Browns, some black, some white, but no person
was so identified as to enable the Court to issue
any process, and, on considering the subject, we
were united in judgment that nothing further
could be done, and I will speak to the Admiral, if
you wish it." And, at his request, the Admiral
set " Brother John" at liberty; and now follows

the words of Moses Brown, of deepest import,—
"It happened well for me and for John that I
knew nothing of his being concerned in the burning of the Gaspee, or that he was charged with
it."

It was his honest entreaty in behalf of "Brother
John," his perfect certainty that John had no connection whatever with the affair, that brought
about his rescue. If anyone is still inclined to
suspect that he knew more than he admitted, par-
ticularly as he was a partner in business with
John, the answer to it is, that we have the words
to the contrary of an honest man, who, of all men,
knew whereof he spoke. He says he not only
knew nothing of John's connection with the affair,
but he did not know "that he was charged with
it." Besides, he had no motive to be false in re-
lating the story voluntarily to Tristam Burges,
sixty years after the event. There was now no
"Brother John" to capture from the merciless
British. It is to be remembered, also, that on
that night, when citizens in the village of Providence were gathering in boats to resist the attack
on their liberties, he was probably at his home by
the Seekonk, more than a mile away, and, as there
was little more than a bridle path to it, that dis-
tance became a far more remote separation than
it would be at present, and hardly a secret in his-

tory was better kept, until there was no further occasion for concealment, than the names of the persons who burnt the Gaspee.

But to return to the brothers: they both mounted the same horse Moses Brown had ridden to Boston, John in the saddle, because he was older and larger, and Moses on behind. They were received upon their arrival in Providence, with joy beyond expression.* They were immediately called upon to attend the General Assembly, and relate all they had seen and heard. Stephen Hopkins, then a member of Congress, was present, and thereupon an earnest discussion ensued, and the Assembly, at that very sitting, voted to raise a regiment of five hundred men, and Generals Greene and Varnum to be put at the head of it.

Moses Brown, having liberated his slaves, became an earnest abolitionist. He was a founder of the Abolition Society of Providence. He gave to the colored people the land† on which they built their house of worship. His house was a place of refuge on the underground railway to Canada. He visited Congress in Philadelphia, asking for the suppression of the slave trade. He agitated the subject constantly in the Society of Friends. They held no slaves themselves, but they were

* See Letter of William Harris.

† Letter to George Macarty, Vol. XIII., p. 32.

urged by him to use everywhere their utmost influence to extinguish the evil. He frequently visited other States, stimulating and spurring the people to legislation against the traffic in men.

Before Garrison and Phillips were born, this excellent man was sturdily fighting the battle of human freedom, with his friends Anthony Benezet* and John Woolman as co-laborers. These men assisted in preparing the way for the final overthrow of that gigantic wickedness. John G. Whittier says, "I read to Moses Brown, in 1833 or 4, at his request, the speech of the Premier on the passage of the Emancipation Act in England." He gave in his will five hundred dollars to the anti-slavery cause.†

Every chapter in the life of this noble man is another illustration of his regard for the whole people, without distinction of race or rank. Vital religion and love to God had filled him with love to men. He had learned the luxury of doing good, and that the highest happiness is found in being helpful to others.

While he labored to free the bodies of one race, he sought by education to liberate the minds of all races and classes.

---

* Benezet wrote that tract which started Thomas Clarkson on his mission to suppress slavery in the British West Indies.

† Letter to Samuel Coates, Vol. XIII., p. 4.

He was appointed, with three others, by the town of Providence, in 1767, to draft an ordinance for free schools, and Higginson says the report of this committee was the first attempt to embody and organize the free school idea.* He was next on a committee of the Society of Friends, in April, 1777, to draw a plan for free schools in the Society, which was carried out, and Moses Brown was placed on the first school committee in northern Rhode Island.

He was deeply interested in Rhode Island College, which afterwards received the name of Brown University. He was a member of the Assembly which granted its charter, and this is given as the reason why he was not a charter member. When Newport, Warren, Greenwich and Providence were all presenting their advantages and special attractions as the abiding place of the college, Stephen Hopkins and Moses Brown were the representatives of Providence in the meeting,

---

* The opening of the first grammar school, was the opening of the first trench against monopoly in Church and State; the first row of trammels and pot-hooks which the little Shearjashubs and Elkanahs blotted and blubbered across their copy-books, was the preamble to the Declaration of Independence.—*Lowell.*

Not only the needle-gun, but the schools, have won our battles.—*Lehnert.*

Public instruction should be the first object of government.—*Napoleon I.*

Toil of Science swells the wealth of Art.—*Schiller.*

and by virtue of their offers of endowment, their eloquence and arguments, the college came to Providence, February 9th, 1770. He gave the college one thousand dollars in 1771, and afterwards a donation of books. Dr. R. A. Guild says: "The first motion to have the college in Providence came, so far as we can learn, from Moses Brown." Is it too much to honor him as a founder of the noble University? He certainly was one of its earnest friends in its infancy.

During the War of the Revolution, the Society of Friends began to agitate the subject of a school for higher education, and in 1780, ten years after the University was located here, a subscription was taken for such a school, and Moses Brown gave five hundred and seventy-five dollars to it. He wrote an earnest appeal to the Society in 1782, of nineteen printed pages, and, in 1784, after the war, the school began, in a little upper chamber in the old meeting house in Portsmouth, R. I. The building is still standing, visible from the hills of Providence, arrayed, it is to be regretted, in modern ornament. His son Obadiah attended this school, and his Latin Grammar, with his name in it, in his father's hand-writing, is kept with miser care. Isaac Lawton, schoolmaster, poet and preacher, was the first principal. This school had a brief life, and after four struggling years, took a recess of thirty-one years.

Moses Brown was treasurer. He gathered the scanty fragments of school property; he invested to advantage, and, in 1814, he offered to donate to the school its present site of forty-three acres of land, and informed the meeting that the remnant of the Portsmouth school estate had grown to nine thousand three hundred dollars. The subscriptions, under this impetus, came in freely, and the school opened again, January 1st, 1819, in the principal building of the present Friends School. He gave the school constant care during the last seventeen years of his life, making perpetual donations to it. His son, Obadiah, died in 1822, leaving to it by far the largest bequest in one sum, which had been given to any school or college in this country.* The will of the boy was in the hand-writing of the father.† They were united to each other as the heart of one man, but the soul of Moses Brown was marching through the history of the Friends School for almost sixty years. It adds to the historic significance of this large fund, that it came from the first manufacture of unmixed cotton fabric in America.

It is neither the time nor the place to consider the importance of this school to Rhode Island and the country. It has sent out thousands upon

---

* Letter of John Osborne, Vol. XIV., p. 292.

† See Letter of Moses Brown, Vol. XIV., p. 288.

thousands of students to influence countless thousands who never saw it. Its founder had the limitations of his sect, as all other people were more circumscribed then than now. I am not sure that they were not quite as unsullied, humane and righteous as we are. He had liberal and broad ideas both as to the means and methods of education. He approved of thorough classical culture.* He wished the advantages of the school to extend beyond the bounds of sect, and to be useful to mankind. Everything he had to do with was planned with a large, far-reaching purpose. It will be remembered, in this connection, that Harvard College, in its beginning, was for Christ and the Church. Its aim was to prepare ministers of the Gospel, but the age and the demands of the times have called it to a wider service.

Moses Brown invited Samuel Slater to come to Providence, and bring with him the Arkwright invention. He was on his way to Philadelphia, and was influenced solely by Moses Brown to come here. Moses Brown selected the Wilkinsons, as the best blacksmiths and mechanics for the undertaking, and it was a very wise choice. They are believed to have been the most skillful in the

---

* "We do not care how much learning our teachers have."—*Letter of Moses Brown to David Daniels, Vol. XIV., p. 319.*

4

country. He had himself been long interested in the subject. He had previously purchased all the machines which he could obtain, that were in the direction of this invention, which invention and undertaking consisted in spinning* cotton so that it could be used for warps in place of linen thread, and in the moving of the machinery by water. It is very important to note how long and how much the mind of Moses Brown was awakened on the subject of cotton spinning before he knew Slater. These previous efforts enable us to see why he so readily took up a stranger, an immigrant without money, drawings, or anything except his own honest, manly person and character to recommend him. It adds greatly to the force of this consideration, if we call to mind that multitudes of imposters had come out from England claiming to be able to construct the Arkwright machinery.

Moses Brown wrote to Samuel Slater, December 12th, 1789: "Come and work our machines, and have the credit as well as advantage of perfecting the first water-mill in America." Samuel Slater came, and Moses Brown took the financial risk, and furnished him with the best means and oppor-

---

* Spinning was performed previously to the year 1767 on the domestic one-thread wheel.—*Memoir of Samuel Slater, by George S. White,* p. 80.

tunity in the country to unfold and perfect the Arkwright invention. Whoever has had his patience tested by the plausible recitals of inventors, or had his bank account depleted in a fruitless attempt to materialize their dreams of impossible things, will have sympathy with the undertaking of Moses Brown, and will entertain a certain reverence for that sublime faith and foresight which controlled and guided him in this great and patriotic service. The eminent services of the Englishman, Samuel Slater, are justly held in high esteem, while the skill, tact, push, and capital of the native Americans, Moses Brown and the Wilkinsons, which so largely contributed to the reconstruction of the machinery here that it seems like a re-invention, are little thought of, or cast off with tardy and scanty praise. They are entitled to a much higher recognition in this country than they have received. It was remarked by one who knew, that the timely practical suggestions of Moses Brown followed the construction at every stage. Moses Brown said, "The machinery was so much longer in preparation than he expected, that he was discouraged."* The most clever and expert mechanics in the world were not then

---

* They were more than a twelve-month completing, before we could get a single warp of cotton perfected.—*Letter of Moses Brown to John Dexter, Oct. 15, 1791, Memoir of Samuel Slater, by George S. White, p. 85.*

swarming in the streets of Providence, neither were huge engines then on every hill and in every valley driving machinery and doing the labor of thousands of men with great perfection and with the versatility almost of human thought. The trials and efforts of Samuel Slater were very great, no doubt. In deep anxiety, with tears in his eyes, he says, "If I am frustrated in my carding machines, they will think me an imposter."* "So great a work it was to found the Roman nation."

Moses Brown, without any aid from the State,† nation, or other persons, carried through and developed, so far as capital was concerned, this art of manufacture, to the great honor and benefit of Rhode Island, an achievement which both the States of Pennsylvania and Massachusetts sought in vain to accomplish with public bounty.

Neither were Moses Brown's trials at an end

* Memoir of Samuel Slater, by George S. White, pp. 96, 97.

† "No encouragement has been given by any laws of this State, nor by any donations of any society or individuals, but wholly begun, carried on, and thus far perfected, at private expense."—*Letter of Moses Brown; see Memoir of Samuel Slater, by George S. White, pp. 88, 89.*

John Dexter has shown his appreciation of the services of Moses Brown in his letter of July 7th, 1791, as follows: "I address myself to you on this subject with more confidence, from a full conviction that, as no one in the State has more at heart the encouragement of our infant manufactures—has been more indefatigable and liberal in the establishment, improvement and use of them than yourself, so no one can possibly possess a more competent knowledge of their commencement, progress and present state."

when the machinery was in successful operation.
When it was known in England that, in spite of
law and of guards, the Arkwright invention had
really escaped and gone to America, then the English manufacturers combined in associations to
flood this country with cheap goods, and, with
bankrupt prices, to strangle the infant at its
birth.*

Then thrice fortunate for this cause and for us,
the tariff of July 4th, 1789, signed by Washington, unconstitutional or not, declared to be for the
assistance of these very industries, came at this
juncture and crisis, as a barrier, protection, and
defence. And also we were fortunate in the cour-
age and steadfast purpose of Moses Brown that,
with profit or without, this should succeed, for the
public good.†

That we may more fully appreciate the scope
and importance of this undertaking, I will quote
from distinguished contemporaries.

Tristam Burges said in Congress,‡ "A circum-

---

*This, I am informed by good authórity, was the policy of the En-
glish manufacturers, formed into societies for that purpose.—MOSES
BROWN.—*Memoir of Samuel Slater, by George S. White, p. 68.*

† "Fire is the test of gold; adversity, of strong men."—*Seneca.*

Grit is the grain of character. It may generally be described as
heroism materialized,—spirit and will thrust into heart, brain, and
backbone, so as to form part of the physical substance of the man.—
*Whipple.*

‡ Speech on the tariff in the House of Representatives, April 21,
1828, p. 80.—See *Memoir of Samuel Slater, by George S. White, p. 94.*

stance worthy of the attention of the whole nation, and worthy, also, of a fair page in history, is the art and mystery of making cloth with machinery moved by water-power. This was introduced into Rhode Island, and commenced at Pawtucket, four miles from Providence, about the same time that the American system of tariff was established by the impost law of July 4th, 1789." * * * "I have often thought Divine Providence directed Slater, and brought him to lay his project before the Wilkinsons, because He had not fitted any other men in the country with minds and abilities either to see and at once comprehend the immense benefit of it, or to understand and perform what must be understood and performed to bring this scheme into full and perfect operation." * * "A yard of cloth made by the wheel and the loom, cost fifty, never less than forty cents; it may now be had for nine or ten cents. A trade so productive of public benefit, will be duly appreciated by all patriots."

I think that we shall all agree, that in a higher, if not a truer sense, Mr. Burges ought to have said, that Divine Providence directed Samuel Slater to Moses Brown, and by years of training and experience, prepared him ardently and joyfully to welcome Mr. Slater. Because the Wilkinsons were only the chosen agents of Moses

Brown, and from the meeting of Brown and Slater, all came as a natural sequence.

Alexander Hamilton, the first Secretary of the Treasury, said in commendation: "The manufactories of cotton goods, not long since established at Beverly, in Massachusetts, and at Providence, in the State of Rhode Island, and conducted with a perseverance corresponding with the patriotic motives which began them, seem to have overcome the first obstacle to success. The quality will bear comparison with the like article brought from Manchester."* But the Secretary does not mention that Beverly, with the bounty and the Commonwealth at its back, still used linen for warps, and was in the rear, far out of sight in the race.

Each of these distinguished contemporaries recognizes the patriotic purpose which dominates this great enterprise, and here, at least, Moses Brown is conspicuous. He says himself, "I, being desirous of perfecting the machines if possible, and the business of cotton manufactures, so as to be useful to the country."

All the other factories† in the country sprang from this one. All the others took the mystery

---

* Report of Alexander Hamilton, Secretary of the Treasury of the United States, December 5, 1791.

† Memoir of Samuel Slater, by George S. White, pp. 106, 107, 85.

and art from this fountain source. To this group
of men, including the Wilkinsons, belongs the
fadeless honor of having begun and set in motion
the elements of that thrift and prosperity in manufacturing with both cotton and wool which has
nourished and built up these New England States,
and provided the people at large with the comforts and luxuries of life, and their homes with
the culture and refinement which characterizes the
highest civilization in the world.*

We will not snatch the laurel from one brow,
to twine it about the other, of these two illustrious
men. One was the father, the other was the foster-parent. The cloth they made could not exist
without both the woof and the warp. This great
achievement required both of them. Let the
praise be duly awarded according to the distinguished merits of each of them, and let all men
join in grateful appreciation of what they did for
us, without us. But let every Rhode Island man,

---

* Tristam Burges said "That these manufactures enabled England so
to multiply labor and accumulate wealth in the close of the last and
beginning of the present century as to stand between the military
despotism of one part of Europe, and the entire liberties of the world."
—*Speech at Pawtucket, June 16, 1828;* see also *Baines' History of Cotton Manufactures.*

"Nor will the enlightened judgment of moderns deny that the
men to whom we owe such inventions, deserve to rank among the
chief benefactors of mankind."—*George S. White's Memoir of Samuel
Slater, p. 91.*

in a special manner, proudly remember that here, on this spot most highly favored of Heaven, the cradle of infant manufactures was first rocked for the whole country.

There was a bit of romance which must not be neglected. When Mr. Slater entered Mr. Wilkinson's house the first time, the blacksmith's daughter disappeared at the same instant by another door, and Mr. Slater's peace of mind went with her. But the course of love met an obstruction. He was not a Friend, and it was a firm rule of the Society then that Friends must not marry other persons. So it was concluded to send Sarah away to school. But the future father of American manufactures said, "You may send her where you please, but I will follow her to the ends of the earth." The contest was hopeless,—the family yielded.

The assistance rendered to Slater by Moses Brown, reminds one of Edward Pease, of England, a Quaker, who, it was said, could see a hundred years ahead. He found George Stephenson, the engine-wright, then known as "Geordie," in a coal pit in the north of England, in 1822. People scoffed, but Pease gave Stephenson capital and opportunity, and the locomotive engine is changing the face of the earth.

It was July 17, 1775, three months after he had

5

liberated "Brother John," that Moses Brown appeared again at the lines of General Washington, in Boston, with a mission to follow in the wasting track of war, and feed the starving poor. Washington could not allow it; the British commanders refused to permit them to pass, but they went to Lynn and sent in provisions in boats, by permission of Admiral Graves.*

Moses Brown, with his committee of Friends, aided three thousand and thirty families in different places, consisting of six thousand nine hundred and twenty-three persons. The Friends of Philadelphia furnished for the purpose $12,700,† in addition to donations in New England. They followed the whole coast from New Hampshire to Newport, including the islands of the sea. These people were not giving aid and comfort to the enemy; they were saving the lives of non-combatants, within the city and without. Such action looks for justification to the higher law, rather than to the will of commanders.‡ It takes its

---

* The latest gospel in this world is, Know thy work, and do it.— *Carlyle.*

Doing good is the only certainly happy action of a man's life.— *Sir Philip Sydney.*

Good deeds ring clear through Heaven, like a bell.—*Richter.*

† Letter of Moses Brown to Henry Loyd, Vol. II., pp. 47, 48, 50. Records of the Yearly Meeting of Friends for New England, 1775.

‡ Humanity is the equity of the heart.—*Confucius.*

appeal to the court of Heaven. Moses Brown was never thought to be disloyal. His philanthropic work was not done in secret. He continued always in the closest friendship with Stephen Hopkins, who was thirty-one years his senior, and was an ardent supporter of the war. Moses Brown writes, in 1781, "I was with Stephen Hopkins sitting, when General Washington called to see him. I sat some time viewing the simple, friendly and pleasant manner in which these two great men met, and conversed with each other on various subjects. I have occasionally seen Washington before and since, and been impressed by his simple, easy manner, as resembling that of Governor Hopkins." The natural inference follows that they both kindly regarded Moses Brown. When President Andrew Jackson visited Providence, June 20th, 1833, he said to him, "I am glad to see thee. I have known all thy predecessors in office, and I wanted to see thee." He was nearly ninety-five years of age then.

The helpful service of this remarkable man appears everywhere in the history of his native city during his long life. He was one of the founders of the Providence Athenæum library; he held share No. 1 in that corporation. He was a founder of a Society for the Promotion of Agriculture in Rhode Island. He was a founder of the Rhode Island Bible Society, an insti-

tution of growing influence. He was a founder
of the Rhode Island Peace Society. He was
also a founder of the Rhode Island Historical
Society, and presided at the organization of this
society, and at the meeting which adopted the
charter.* We have already mentioned that he
was a founder of the Abolition Society, the mission of which has fortunately passed away. He
was a charter member of several of these institutions, and if we add his connection with the College and the Friends School, we have a worthy
exhibition of his quickening and vitalizing influence in this community. The historical service
rendered by him was not, however, limited to the
Historical Society. If you would study the early
commerce and shipping of the port of Providence,
the most trustworthy original document, is a letter
of Moses Brown. If you are interested in the
great storm which, in the year 1815, nearly sub-
merged Providence, the best account of it is in a
letter of Moses Brown. If you wish to study the
history of the University, or other institutions in
Providence, or the character and achievements of
his distinguished contemporaries for almost a century, the reliable side-light on the subject is everywhere found in a letter from Moses Brown.† It

---

* See Circular, Vol. XIV.; Letters, p. 284.

† The voluminous extant correspondence of Moses Brown, assures us

seems proper and needful, if we would thoroughly appreciate him, that we should follow him more closely still, into his personal and home life.*

I think he began his married life at what was known as the "Neck Farm," opposite the Swan Point Cemetery, and it was his confident expectation to have remained there the rest of his days, in retirement, but in about 1770, he bought of the executor of the will of John Merritt, the "Elm Grove Farm," near Red Bridge. He built the first bridge, and here he had his home until the end of life.† A home around which clusters great historic interests. He paid six thousand dollars for this broad domain, where Mr. Merritt, a princely Englishman, with the true instincts of an Englishman, dwelt remote from town on his landed estate. Mr. Merritt had the proud distinction of having, if not the first, certainly at one period, the only coach in Providence, and when this coach came into the street by way of Olney's Lane, the children attended it with the same

of his wide personal influence, both public and private. It includes letters to and from the foremost men of his period, upon a great variety of subjects.—See *Letters of Moses Brown to George Washington, John Hancock, and others,* in the Cabinet of the R. I. Historical Society.

It is also worthy of note, that he did a great service for very many families, by collecting and preserving their genealogical records. —See *Genealogical Papers of Moses Brown,* R. I. Historical Society.

* Home is the sacred refuge of our life.—*Dryden.*

† Letter of George W. Peck, Vol. XIII., pp. 4 and 5.

eagerness with which they greet a modern show. Mary, the sister of Mr. Brown's wife, took the farm which he left, but in 1771 he carried a small elm tree on his back from Cat Swamp and planted it before the door of his first home. This tree is still, at the age of more than one hundred and twenty years, hale and hearty.* Multitudes of happy people have mingled in the festivities and merry-makings under its spreading branches and grateful shade, cooling themselves with ice-cream, and entertaining themselves regally with that berry of which Dr. William Butler said, "Doubtless God could have made a better berry, but doubtless God never did," a sentiment approved in the "Complete Angler," and by mankind generally. This tree extends a hundred and fifteen feet from one extremity to the other, one of the largest trees in the State. It still flourishes in pride and beauty, a stately and magnificent emblem of the noble institutions he planted. It will have crumbled to dust when they, in the vigor of their usefulness will be still spreading aloft over men their beneficent influence.

Moses Brown retired early from business, be-

---

* Old trees, in their living state, are the only things that money cannot command.—*Landor.*

A tree is a nobler object than a prince in his coronation robes.—*Pope.*

cause he was afflicted with a fearful vertigo, which attended him all his life, and must have seriously interrupted the plans, purposes and activity of such a man. His own infirmities led him to give thoughtful attention to disease in every form, and to the remedies. An extensive knowledge of medicine thus acquired, rendered him, when good physicians were scarce, exceedingly useful to his neighbors.* He was constantly consulted, and freely administered both advice and medicines.† He was fond of mathematical study, and found in Stephen Hopkins a kindred spirit in these delightful fields. He gave constant attention to physics and chemistry. He sought in every way to put to practical and daily use all that he saw and read. The roof of his carriage was covered with white material, to resist and not attract the heat of the sun. He had extensive physical apparatus, and materials for chemical experiments always at hand.

The home at "Elm Grove" was the abode constantly of a deep, sincere spiritual life. And this is the root and ground of the influence which everywhere emanates from this saintly man. He never himself posed as a saint, and for that reason we are more inclined to believe he was one. His

* Letter of Jessie Howard, Vol. XIV., p. 285.

† Letter of M. Rotch, Vol. XIII., p. 7.

life seems to centre on the two Commandments, on which "hang all the law and the prophets," Love to God and Love to man. He and his religious associates laid great stress upon personal, supernatural, Divine, spiritual guidance. The command to set free his slaves was an instance in point, of this illumination. The Friends were highly charged also with the Puritanic hostility to the superfluity and vanity-fair of this world, which consumes the lives of men in a perpetual round of folly.* They felt that "Life is real, life is earnest," a solemn truth, as vital to-day as ever. It is important, however, to note that circumstances alter cases, and that many things which in that day would have been luxurious and extravagant, even for the rich, the use of machinery has made almost essential in the humblest home. There is now leisure and money for art, which did not exist when the struggle for bare subsistence was so fierce and doubtful. The elements which determine what is extravagance, change from age to age, but the testimony against it when recognized, ought to be perpetual.

Moses Brown was no ascetic. He thankfully received and used every reasonable creaturely comfort. Four meals a day, the year round, was the

---

* It is the age that forms the man, not the man that forms the age.
—*Macaulay.*

rule at "Elm Grove." Breakfast at eight o'clock, dinner at one, tea at five or six, and supper at nine, and to bed at ten o'clock. He was a moderate eater, and selected his food more with regard to health than to appetite. He was very hospitable; he often had twenty or thirty guests at a time to lodge at his house. It was full indeed, sometimes to overflowing. It is related that on one occasion, finding himself perplexed to furnish beds for his guests, he entered the room and said, "Friends, we shall have to make Shaking Quakers of you, and separate the men from the women, to give you all beds."

He was for very many years a venerated patriarch and peace-maker in this neighborhood.* If any man or woman had a quarrel or perplexity, they taxed the patience and sought the judicial wisdom of Moses Brown, through almost three generations. His correspondence, contained in eighteen well-bound volumes in this cabinet, shows that his life must have been heavily burdened with the troubles of persons who sought advice and assistance constantly. He rarely, if ever failed, so far as we know, to do the right thing in the right way, to say the right word at the right time. Sometimes attempts were made to impose

---

* See Letter of Phebe Fenner, Vol. XIV., p. 285; Zebedee Hopkins, Vol. XIII., p. 30; Mary C. Waterman, p. 31.

on his good nature, and the scathing lightning of his displeasure would frown the person out of his presence, rebuked and discomfited. When occasion required, he spoke his convictions. The habitual expression of his face was pensive, but not sad. Conspicuous in his character were goodness, generosity, charity, and wisdom. He was, as Sir John Denham said of Father Thames,

"Though deep, yet clear, though gentle, yet not dull,
Strong without rage, without o'erflowing, full."

He was retiring, never self-asserting. He would not have his picture painted, and it was taken without his knowledge. He had no sympathy with persons who did good works to appear unto men. They should be done, he thought as a duty to God, and to men, with little or no mixture of selfishness.

There is something very admirable in a builder, author, or anybody else, who, in self-forgetfulness, labors for the good of remote generations, which can never reward his service, whether it be to plant a tree by the wayside, or write a book, or paint a picture, or design the Cathedral at Cologne.* Unselfishness anywhere and everywhere,

* There cannot be a more glorious object in creation than a human being, replete with benevolence, meditating in what manner he might render himself most acceptable to his Creator, by doing most good to his creatures.—*Fielding.*

You will find people ready enough to do the Samaritan without the oil and two pence.—*Sydney Smith.*

is God-like. It is such, even in battle. The homage of mankind has attended the memory of that poor common soldier who saved the life of Sydney on the field of Marston Moor, and, when found that he might be rewarded, refused to give his name, saying, " It was not for that I did it."

No one was allowed to paint his picture, and no one was encouraged to write his biography. Had he been a religious minister, the work of the Lord might have been spread out on the printed page, but not the outward career of the poor unworthy creature himself.*

We live in another age, under another gospel. When all men are taught to make this world appear to blossom as the rose, while not neglecting the next, or themselves, and that all human greatness, goodness, and nobility should be held aloft by the just themselves, for the reasonable admiration and imitation of mankind.

The moral heroes are the greatest. There are marked distinctions in great men. One order of leaders, like Cæsar or Bonaparte, seem to use their gifts exclusively for their own emolument or personal advantage.† Another, like Lincoln,

---

* The humble soul is like the violet, which grows low, hangs the head downward, and hides itself with its own leaves.—*Frederika Bremer.*

† If I am asked who is the greatest man, I answer, The best; and

Washington, and the entire army of philanthropic
men, have sought to be of use to men, to improve
the conditions of human existence.

And to this end they have taken greater personal risks of life, property, and reputation, and
have bravely stood, like the heroes of Thermopylæ,
in the pass where the battle of ideas, of intellec-
tual and spiritual freedom, as well as personal liberty, was to be struggled for in behalf of mankind.

Quiet, unnoticed, but steadfast, able heroes, who
counted no cost too dear, no suffering too great to
be endured, in the service of their fellow-men.

Moses Brown belongs to this noble class of
moral greatness and grandeur. And let his own
State be proud of him. He is "to the manner
born." He drew the elements that made up his
grand character from this vicinity. His life has
the flavor of the soil of Rhode Island. The same
which produced the great and saintly Channing,
the eloquent, incorruptible and matchless Curtis.
It is not a small matter to have lived almost a
century, and to have been so guided by intellect
and moved by high moral sense, as to stand at
the end of so long an exposure to the eyes of men,

if I am required to say who is the best, I reply, He that has deserved
the most of his fellow-creatures.—*Sir W. Jones.*

I believe the first test of a truly great man is his humility.—*Ruskin.*

still true, just, noble, sustaining a moral character without a flaw.

It has been a great misfortune to many a one that he lived too long, and survived his usefulness; but here was a man who "husbanded out life's taper to the close," "And, although his days were many, the very last were rich and eventful." He seemed to descend the declivity of old age without a consciousness of decay.*  He never for a moment lost his interest in things about him, spiritual or secular, to the very closing hour of life.  Multitudes of his friends had passed away, and there he stood like an ancient oak on the mountain side, towering above later generations, serene, majestic, unclouded.

He changed his will several times a little before his death, without the least indication of loss of mental power.

He withdrew for many years, more and more from the society of the world, to the sacred companionship of the same religious faith.

The sectarian fences were higher and more bitterly guarded then.  The grand unity of Christianity was less known and felt than now.  There was one lessening circle of kindred spirits which grew constantly dearer and more interesting to the very close of his life.  One theme and one

---

* See Letter of Joseph E. Worcester, Vol. XIV., p. 283.

purpose united them into holy sympathy and tender fellowship.* This was not the withered and hideous old age depicted by Montaigne, when he said, "Age imprints more wrinkles in the mind than it does on the face; and souls are never, or very rarely seen, that, in growing old, do not smell sour and musty. Man moves all together, both towards his perfection and decay." Did Montaigne overlook the sweetness and light which spring from a correspondence fixed with Heaven through the growing years? Did he not know it is possible for both body and intellect to waste away and the spirit meanwhile to grow stronger, clearer, deeper and nearer to the Eternal, even to the end, and that it is the Divine Spirit which sends the "Gulf Stream of Youth into the Arctic Region of our lives?"† "But the path of the just is as the shining light that shineth more and more unto the perfect day."

A poet who had known and felt it all, says more sweetly and truly, "Age is opportunity, no less than youth itself, though in another dress, and as the evening twilight fades away, the sky is filled with stars invisible by day."‡

This poet has beautifully delineated in these

---

* Letter of John Griscom, Vol. XIV., p. 286.

† The youth of the soul is everlasting, and eternity is youth.—*Richter*.

‡ Henry Wadsworth Longfellow.

picturesque lines the daily life experience and faith of Moses Brown.

Thomas Jefferson wrote his own epitaph, "The Author of the Declaration of Independence; of the Statute of Virginia for Religious Freedom; and the Father of the University of Virginia." But here is a life-work of greater depth and compass than the composition of Statutes or Declarations of Liberty. It embraced freedom for the colored man, manufacturing industry, patriotism, education, philanthropy. No marble shaft towers above his grave in the old North Burying Ground. No mausoleum points to his abode among the rich and great. The brief stories of his birth and death are legible on a small unattractive stone, almost lost to sight in that wide field of sorrow, not far from the grave of his honored and beloved friend, Stephen Hopkins.

But he has set in fadeless colors the influence of his useful life-work on these hills and valleys. His monument is about us. Wherever commerce, wherever the arts and humanities touch and ennoble the race, Moses Brown is present, though his name may not pass from lip to lip.*

> "Fear not but that thy light once more shall burn,
> Once more thine immemorial gleam return."
>
> —*Matthew Arnold.*

* When good men die, their goodness does not perish; but lives though they are gone.—*Euripides.*